Maggie

**Other books by
Ann M. Martin**

Leo the Magnificat
Rachel Parker, Kindergarten Show-off
Eleven Kids, One Summer
Ma and Pa Dracula
Yours Turly, Shirley
Ten Kids, No Pets
Slam Book
Just a Summer Romance
Missing Since Monday
With You and Without You
Me and Katie (the Pest)
Stage Fright
Inside Out
Bummer Summer

THE KIDS IN MS. COLMAN'S CLASS series
BABY-SITTERS LITTLE SISTER series
THE BABY-SITTERS CLUB mysteries
THE BABY-SITTERS CLUB series
CALIFORNIA DIARIES series

California Diaries #3

Maggie

Ann M. Martin

SCHOLASTIC INC.
New York Toronto London Auckland Sydney

ISBN 0-590-29837-2

12 11 10 9 8 7 6 5 4 3 2 1   7 8 9/9 0 1/0

Printed in the U.S.A   40

First Scholastic printing, October 1997

The author gratefully acknowledges
Peter Lerangis
for his help in
preparing this manuscript.

Maggie

I am
~~I'm~~ yesterday's girl
wearing   smile,
~~In~~ yesterday's ~~clothes~~

singing yesterday's songs
can you stay here awhile
~~While the evening light goes~~
'cause
~~And~~ I don't see tomorrow
No,
~~'cause~~ I'm yesterday's girl.

© Maggie Blume

Sunday 11/9
10:43 A.M.

God, that is sad.
No, sad isn't the word.
Bad.
That's what it is. Bad.
Awful.
Who ever told me I could be a
songwriter?

No one. Just myself.

I was wrong.

Monday 11/10
5:57 P.M.

Feeling better today. Even though (1) I have tons of homework, (2) I am about to flunk Wednesday's math test, and (3) dinner is delayed because Dad is arguing on the phone with some studio exec about his upcoming movie, *Fatal Judgment* (which may be one of his worst ever, judging from the rough cut we saw).

The reason I am feeling better is this:

At 3:50 P.M., during *Inner Vistas* elections after school, I, Maggie Blume, was chosen as poetry editor. I remember the time because I was staring at the clock, trying not to look jittery. Parker Price, the editor-in-chief, announced I was the first eighth-grader ever elected to the editorial staff. (Not so impressive, considering this is the first year Vista eighth-graders have been switched to the high school building.) After the election, Parker told me she hopes I'll take over as editor-in-chief someday. Now, THAT was impressive.

Magazine editor. The more I think about it, the more I like the idea. For my life's work.

It's perfect. Get paid to read. Judge other people's writing and tell them what to do. Launch the careers of talented writers. Hire a music reviewer so the magazine can receive free CDs from record company PR departments.

This is almost as good an idea as becoming a veterinarian (which is what I'll probably decide to be).

I swear I am going to be the best editor *Inner Vistas* has ever seen. When I'm editor-in-chief, who knows? Maybe I'll lead us to a national award.

Then the sky's the limit.

I just have to remember not to tell Dad. He'd decide to manage my career. He'd have the presidents of all the major magazine companies over for dinner, just to meet me. He'd make me recite my poems. Sing my lyrics. Show how I edit, using an overhead projector.

He might even forget about making me play my latest piano piece for all his guests.

That, at least, would be a relief.

Where would I be without laptops? I am so glad Vista allows them in the classroom.

Ms. Newell has given us 15 minutes of independent work time. She thinks we're all typing our book reports. But I finished last night. So I have plenty of time to write in my journal.

Thought for the day:

Sunny Winslow is a high-maintenance friend. These days, you give her a lot more than you get.

It's hard enough dealing with this rebel phase she's in. I mean, I *know* what she's going through. The black lipstick, weird hair, funky clothes — *been there*.

But for me it was a stage. *I* never had

body piercings. I never cut school. And I never shut myself off from my friends. You can't even talk to her anymore. She's in another world.

I thought she was coming out of it today at lunch. She sat right down with Dawn and me, all friendly and excited.

But then I learned the reason. She wanted to show me her copy of *Variety,* with every mention of Dad's name highlighted.

I tried to be polite. But how many times can I stand reading the ads for *Fatal Judgment*?

When she was the old Sunny, I never minded her starry-eyed attitude about the movie business. She thought it was so cool that we had intercoms in every room. Infrared burglar sensors. The landscaped pool. Movie people visiting the house all the time. All my private at-home lessons. Never mind that the alarms go off by themselves in the middle of the night. Or that Dad holds loud poolside meetings outside my bedroom window. Or that I have to play piano all the time for strangers in power suits. Or that Dad's mood swings go up and down with the box office grosses. And so does Mom's drinking.

I even showed Sunny that pathetic photo of me as a newborn, with the words A HAYDEN BLUME PRODUCTION taped onto my bassinet. She thought that was cool too.

But Sunny was always so much fun to be with. If she thought my life was glamorous, fine. However, since she's decided to be Punk Dropout of the Year, I'm having much less patience with her.

Now she also thinks she's a casting director. *Variety* decided to print the casting notice of Dad's NEXT film, even though *Fatal Judgment* hasn't opened yet. Right there in the cafeteria, Sunny read aloud one of the character descriptions — something like, *Male, late teens, dark, drop-dead handsome, young Pierce Brosnan features with Harrison Ford swagger.*

She announced that only one person in the world was destined to play the role.

Yes. Justin Randall.

Here we go again.

One time in my life I just *happen* to mention I *think* he's good-looking. (And he IS.

Anyone would agree.) But it's an OBSERVATION. Like judging a work of art.

Not to Sunny, however. To Sunny it is a declaration of love.

Sunny made sure to point out he's a *junior.* And he has a *car.* Then she warned that I should not "blow this opportunity." But of course I shouldn't make it easy for him either. "Let him twist in the wind," advised Sunny. "Tell him you *may* let your dad audition him. Seduce him. Then call me right away with the details."

Seduce him.

I could not believe her. I mean, the nerve.

I should have told her off. But I didn't. I was chicken. I said something stupid like, "Dad is looking for professional actors only."

Sunny had an answer for that too. She told me Justin played "the Gentleman Visitor" in last year's high school production of *The Glass Monastery.* Plus he's dying to be a movie star *and* he has head shots.

I did not tell her the character was "Gentleman *Caller*" and the play was *The Glass*

Menagerie. I did not want to lengthen the ridiculous conversation.

Good old Dawn the Peacemaker was trying valiantly to change the subject. She kept remarking about how healthy the new vegetarian menu is. She made a few cracks about how the entire school reeks whenever the cafeteria serves beef. Typical Dawn stuff. But it wasn't working. Sunny wouldn't give up. "You have the perfect opening line, Maggie. 'Wanna come home and meet my dad, the famous movie producer?' I wish it were that easy for me. Not in this life. I mean, 'Wanna meet my dad, the bookstore owner, and my mom, who's dying of cancer?' just doesn't have that same ring."

This is so typical. Just when I'm about to lose my temper, she reminds me of her problems. And I feel bad for her, because her problems really are serious, so how can I possibly be angry? On the other hand, she throws the problems in my face, so I can't exactly sympathize either.

So I babbled clichés. I told her to think positive. And, of course, I felt guilty.

But I was beginning to develop a theory.

Maybe *Sunny* was interested in Justin Randall. I mean, it's *possible.* Sunny's unattached. And she *does* like older guys. That guy she met at the beach — Carson — he was a high school dropout.

Okay, let's say my theory is true. She's in love. But Justin's not too interested. After all, Sunny's only thirteen.

So Sunny must find a way to get close. Something that separates her from the average eighth-grader.

So she says: "I happen to know the daughter of Hayden Blume, the movie producer, who just happens to be looking to discover a new star, in a role that just happens to be perfect for you. . . ."

What's the next logical step? She tries to arrange an audition, through me. And what's the best way to convince me to do it? To make me think she's matching *me* up.

Maybe she's just getting to Justin *through* me.

Would she be so devious? *Sunny,* who used to be one of my best friends?

I wouldn't put it past her.

What do I care if Sunny's being sneaky? Why am I even *thinking* about it? Especially on a night before a math exam that I know I will flunk.

If Sunny wants Justin Randall, fine. She has every right to pursue him. Just as I have every right not to listen to her advice about inviting him for an audition.

Period. End of discussion.

The strange thing was, I spotted Justin in the hallway right after lunch. And then later, between classes.

And I couldn't help thinking, he *would* actually be right for that part.

If I cared.

Which I don't.

I saw you today,
            through,
You looked right ~~past~~ me.
What's in those eyes?

Tell me, what do you see?
We are closer than close,
But we're so far away.
My heart says, "~~You must~~ Go ahead,"
But my mind tells me, "stay,"
            my wildest dream,
Ohhhh, not in ~~this life,~~
Not in this life,
        enter   mind   cut
You ~~come into~~ my ~~brain~~ and ~~twist~~ like a knife,
        feel all alone,
Now I'~~m hung out to dry~~
And I'm twistin' in the wind...

Wednesday 11/12
lunch period

Got a 94 on my math test.
Two problems wrong. Easy ones.
Stupid, stupid, stupid mistakes.

$$100$$
$$95$$
$$99$$
$$100$$
$$\underline{94}$$
$$488/5 = 97.6 \text{ avg.}$$

One more test before the end of the marking period. If I get a 100 I can pull my average up to 588/6 = 98. The final counts double, of course, so a 100 on *that* would make it 788/8 = 98.5.

If I could average in what I *really* got on that first test — 105 with the bonus points — I'd already be at 98.6. Ms. Sevekow keeps saying she doesn't believe in counting bonus points into your average if they gave you over a 100 test score. Fine. So why won't she let me *transfer* the points to another test? Like, bring the 94 up to a 99? That is so unfair. But I can't argue about it. There are enough nerds in the class who *would,* and I am not one of them.

I'll just have to do better next time.

Wednesday
5:17 P.M.

Why are my fingers SO STIFF?

Something must be wrong with me. Maybe I'm coming down with arthritis.

Maybe it's not me. Maybe it's Mrs. Knudsen. She assigned me the Beethoven

"Pathétique Sonata" on purpose. She knew I couldn't possibly play it. She knows my fingers can't handle so many notes.

She's trying to make me quit. That way she won't have to listen to all my clinkers anymore.

Listen to me. I am feeling so sorry for myself. Even Curtis (such a good cat) seems sick of my complaining. I don't even have to say anything — he just *knows*.

I just need to practice more. That's all. Plus I have to insist on pieces that are more fun. Classical's nice, but once in a while I want to jump forward to this century.

Next week I'll give Mrs. Knudsen an ultimatum. I'll agree to learn Beethoven if she agrees to teach me the blues.

On piano, that is.

A knock on the door. Got to go.

Wednesday
9:46 P.M.

The good news: That knock was Dad.

He was home early from work. Which is pretty amazing, considering *Fatal Judgment* opens in three weeks. At this point, he's usually in the office 24 hours a day.

The bad news: He had heard every minute of my piano lesson.

And that was what he wanted to talk about.

"So, practicing enough, honey?" he asked.

I said no. I told him how busy I'd been — math test, book report, and so on.

He nodded. He told me he'd just beaten Carlton Grant in tennis.

"You always beat him," I said.

"That's because I keep up my game," Dad replied. "No matter how busy I am, no matter how many meetings I take, nothing stands in the way of my tennis game. Why? Because it's my passion, Maggie. Always make time for your passion."

At first I had no idea what he was talking about. Then I realized.

"You mean, I should practice piano more," I said.

Dad nodded. "You do enjoy it, don't you? I mean, I hope I haven't been paying Mrs. Knudsen for eight years in vain."

Why does he always bring this up?

I reassured him. I said I enjoyed lessons. I promised I'd practice more.

But he still had this strange, super-concerned look. "This Dustin fellow? Is he — are you and he —?"

Dustin.

Dustin Hoffman?

"What are you talking about?" I asked.

"Sunny just called. I didn't get you because you were in the middle of your lesson. She mentioned this fellow . . ."

Justin.

Dad was asking me if Justin and I were going out.

Why? Because Sunny had gushed about him. And she'd asked if I had mentioned him yet.

And somehow Dad got the idea that I had a crush on him.

I was so humiliated.

How could she do this?

I explained everything to Dad. I told him about my lunch conversation with Sunny. I explained that I didn't know Justin.

Dad nodded. But he still had that concerned look. "Mind if we talk a bit,

Maggie? I was sitting in the kitchen, listening to you play, and I thought: Maybe she needs to branch out. Something more than just piano lessons. A school activity. You'd still have plenty of time to practice."

I reminded him of my extracurriculars. Honor Society. *Inner Vistas.*

"*What* Vistas?" he asked.

I know I've explained *Inner Vistas* to him. But when I told him it was a literary magazine, and I explained I was poetry editor, he seemed to be hearing it for the first time.

He barely even acknowledged it. It was as if I'd told him I was on the school wallpaper committee or something. Right away he asked me if I'd be interested in joining Drama Club.

"You know I don't like show business," I said.

"Just checking," Dad replied. "Interests change. Anyway, you do like music, right? How about the school orchestra?"

I told him that wasn't a bad idea, but I was happy doing just what I'm doing now.

His face got really serious. He said I needed to think about college. According to him, "the top-drawer schools" want more than excellent grades. They want interesting, involved kids with lots of extracurriculars.

"You have to work up to your best ability," he said. "Because you'll be competing shoulder-to-shoulder with other kids who are. And now that you're in high school, it's a good time to start."

I reminded him I was not in high school. Just in the high-school *building.*

"I don't want to split hairs," Dad said. "Most eighth-graders are already putting their five-year plans in order."

Five-year plan?

I never heard of such a thing. But Dad knows all about it. He had one.

When Dad was my age, he was already making films. Which was one of the reasons he got into UCLA. Which put him on the road to future success. He's told me that a hundred times.

Well, *I'm* not going into filmmaking,

that's for sure. No matter how much he tries to convince me. Someday I want to say to him, "Look what *I've* done."

Maybe I'll head up a magazine someday. Or establish my own. Or publish a book of poems. Or be a veterinarian. *Who knows?*

Dad is right about one thing. I'll need to go to a great college. But for *my* reasons. To follow *my* road to success, using *my* talents.

If I need extra activities to do that, fine. I'll join some.

Tomorrow I can talk to Mr. Pearson about orchestra.

Thursday morning, 11/13
Too early

Chains
Prison   confine
capture.
Chamber   Skin   shell ←
Tough. But breakable. Thin/hard

It's lonely in here
But it's lonely outside

Get me out of this shell
No, I don't wanna hide
Wanna fly...
Wanna feel the air beneath my wings
~~Wanna taste the air~~
But I'm locked up in here
In this shell that I'm in
My home, my mind, my body
Me, myself, and I.

or something like that.
I have to go to school.
to be continued

Thursday
lunchtime

Got to write fast. Get my thoughts down before lunch chat starts. Dawn's in line, which means she'll be sitting here any minute.

Talked to Mr. Pearson in the orchestra room before homeroom. Told him I wanted to join the orchestra.

His reaction? He danced.

"Hallelujah, a volunteer!" he said. Then he asked what instrument I play.

"Piano," I said.

Droop went his smile. He explained the piano is more of a solo instrument. Used in concertos and chamber music, which the school orchestra doesn't play.

I sort of knew that, but I hadn't thought it through. I felt like such a fool.

Then he asked if I play anything else, so I told him guitar.

"Sorry," he said. "Not in the orchestra either. But we do have a spot for a sousaphone player."

That sounded cool. I asked what that looked like.

He pointed to a tuba.

Thanks but no thanks.

In the hallway after first period I saw Mr. Schildkraut, who runs the school newspaper. I figured, *why not?* As long as I'm not going to be in orchestra.

But he said editorial positions are filled.

He suggested submitting an article. Maybe I'll do that. If I can think of a topic.

I'll ask Dawn what she thinks.

More later.

Done with math homework. Now I can write in this until I have to go to English.

Okay. I *must* write about what happened at lunch.

We did not get off to a good start. When I told Dawn about my meeting with Mr. Pearson, she suggested I learn the flügelhorn. (Frankly, I think she just likes the sound of the name.)

Soon Sunny sat with us, looking very distracted (and VERY tan). Her suggestion?

"Join the chorus!"

I nearly burst out laughing. I sound like a sick moose when I sing.

Sunny just shrugged and said, "So? The guys in the bass section are cute. That's all that really matters."

Dawn told me I have a great voice. She pointed out that I'm always going around singing.

"Yeah, with people who won't laugh at me," I replied, "like you. Besides, the only songs I like are rock. Pop. R&B. The chorus is so . . . formal."

"So's the stuff you play on piano," Sunny remarked.

"That's different," I said. "I'm used to it. Mrs. Knudsen's been teaching me that music since I was five."

Then Sunny suggested I volunteer to play piano for the school musical.

Dawn shook her head. "We'd have to assassinate Mrs. Dunlap. She's been playing for the musicals since my dad was a student here."

Dawn kept on trying to think of ideas — French Club, Astronomy Club, cheerleading squad. Sunny, however, started making fun of me. Telling me I should take up surfing. Intermediate coed lip wrestling. Typical juvenile sense of humor.

When I asked her to be serious, she called me a nerd.

I almost lost my temper. But I didn't want to cause a scene so I just stayed silent. She kept talking about the book she's reading — *On the Road.* It's like her bible. (I wonder if surf-boy Carson introduced her to that.)

On the way out of the cafeteria, Sunny began twanging air guitar and singing "RESPECT." (She knows I love Aretha.)

Then Dawn began singing along too. Both of them put their arms around my shoulders, sandwiching me.

"Come on, Maggie, sing!" Sunny said.

I was way too embarrassed. I shook my head.

But the halls were pretty crowded. No one was even looking at Dawn and Sunny.

They were getting to the best part of the song. And I was dying to join in. So I did. Softly.

But you can't really sing "RESPECT" softly. You kind of have to let it all out at the end.

Well, when we reached the loudest part, we were under that dome-shaped area in the ceiling. Our voices sounded incredibly loud there. I could not believe it. It must have been a natural echo or something.

Anyway, it was really embarrassing, so

we stopped. But now people *were* staring at us.

One of them was Amalia Vargas. She started applauding.

"Aretha!" she called out.

"You like her?" Sunny asked.

Amalia nodded. "You sound great."

Well, I figured she was talking about all of us. So I just nodded.

But Dawn said, "That's what we've been trying to tell her."

"Did you ever sing in a band?" Amalia asked.

That was when I realized Amalia was looking straight at me.

I nearly burst out laughing.

"Seriously," Amalia said. "You're good."

Well, I barely know Amalia. I thought maybe she had some weird sense of humor. Or she was musically challenged.

But Dawn and Sunny were agreeing with her. And I was convinced they all were crazy.

Amalia started talking excitedly about some upcoming Battle of the Bands. It's going to be at this coffeehouse called Backstreet. She said she's "more or less going out" with a guy, James, who's in one of the competing bands, called Vanish.

I tuned out after awhile because I was worried I'd be late for class.

"Would you be interested?" Amalia asked.

I thought she meant, would I be interested in seeing them. So I said sure.

"Great!" Amalia exclaimed. "Show them a ballad and something really raw."

"Huh?" I said.

"For the audition."

"You want me to audition?"

"Duh," Sunny muttered.

"The backup singer just quit," Amalia explained. "They're going to need a new one."

I told Amalia no way. Politely.

"If you change your mind, let me know," Amalia said.

She ran off, and I headed toward class with Sunny and Dawn.

They were both mad at me. Dawn said I should be proud of my voice.

Sunny wasn't as gentle. She accused me of being too worried about homework. She thought *that* was the reason I'd said no.

"Bring your homework to rehearsals," she said. "Get *James* to help you. He's pretty cute."

(Honestly, that girl is possessed. Isn't Justin enough for her?)

"You wanted another after-school activity, right?" Dawn asked. "This would be perfect for you."

I couldn't help laughing. I could just see how Dad would react to that. He would freak.

Which was almost enough to make me consider it.

I mean, I love Dad and all, but I am not his little puppet.

Still.

You really have to *sing* to be in a band.

"I meant a *school* activity," I said. "Something that goes on your record."

Sunny let out this little scream of frustration. "What has *happened* to you, Maggie? You are so . . . straight! Girl, you need to loosen up!"

I did not smack her.

But I wanted to.

The weird thing is, I've been daydreaming ever since then about being

Aretha Franklin. Singing in front of a huge crowd at the Kingdome.

It's ridiculous, I know. But it would be fun. In another life.

POSS. NEWSPAPER ARTICLES/(COLUMNS?)

Interview with Mr. Pearson. His education and what he really wanted to do before becoming a

Polling Place — Student polls on issues of the day

Screenings — Movie reviews (maybe title too obscure?)

Music Muse — CD reviews

Confessions of a Movie Brat. An inside look at the film industry. Start with coverage of the *Fatal Judgment* premiere?

I hate these.

Well, maybe the last one's okay. I can take notes at the screening.

It'll keep me from being bored to death.

Horrible, horrible night.

Dad is at the studio.

Mom is all upset.

Pilar may have quit working for us.

Zeke is in the dumps. He's also in the doghouse.

When Dad called, Zeke picked up the phone and started yelling at him. Apparently Dad had forgotten he was supposed to take Zeke out for ice cream.

After Zeke hung up, he accidentally-on-purpose knocked a bowl and a glass onto the floor. Pilar was not happy.

Big fight. Zeke called Pilar all kinds of names and stomped outside.

I was doing homework when Mom let out a scream like I've never heard before.

She'd found Zeke floating in the pool facedown.

He has played this trick a million times already. Not with Mom, though, I guess.

By the time I got downstairs, Zeke was

swimming around, laughing. Mom looked as if she'd had a heart attack. She screamed at Zeke. Then she yelled at Pilar. She complained that Pilar should be keeping an eye on Zeke.

"He is eleven years old," Pilar said. "He is not a baby."

Well, Mom and Pilar started arguing. Pilar said housekeeping is taking too much out of her and she needs her energy for acting class.

Mom told Pilar she needs *money* for acting class. That is such a Dad thing to say. I was shocked to hear it from Mom.

Pilar must have been shocked too. She walked out in a huff.

I holed up in my bedroom and finished all my homework before dinner — which I had to cook because Pilar did not come back. (Mom wanted to order take-out pizza, but I'm sick of that.) I did not dare ask Mom whether Pilar had quit. I could tell that subject was off-limits.

I hate when Dad's schedule gets busy like this. My family turns into such a soap opera.

Things are quieter now. Still tense, though. I can hear Mom's voice. She's in her room, talking angrily on the phone with Dad.

I think Zeke has fallen asleep in front of the TV.

He's lucky. I'm wired. Not sleepy a bit.

You snap your fingers
Pick up the phone
A word or two
What you want is done.
I hear you say "Jump."
Someone ~~says~~ answers, "How high?"
Tell me, are you happy
In your corner of the sky?
'cause life can change
When you least expect it.
It ain't a movie
And you can't direct it.
And someday soon,
You've gotta make room,
'cause there's space up there,
For my own share
~~In~~ Of that corner of the sky.

© Maggie Blume

Friday morning
11/14

I hardly slept.

Dad did not come home last night. Mom said he camped out on his office sofa.

Zeke is sick. Mom's angry because she has to stay home with him.

And Pilar has quit.

I cannot wait to go to school. Anything to get out of this house.

Friday
math class

She thinks she knows me. But she doesn't.

Sunny thinks that by digging into me, she'll make me change. She'll make me be more like HER.

That's why she wants me to sing in that band. It has nothing to do with what *I* want. It has nothing to do with what would be best for *me.*

No. Sunny thinks only about Sunny. She wants to live *through* me.

I'm sorry, I'm in no mood for her today. At our lockers she had the nerve to tell me I needed to "take a walk on the wild side."

I wanted to say, "Yeah, when pigs fly."

She can walk on the wild side. She can drop out of school and run away. She can do whatever she wants.

Where's she going to end up? What's she going to do for a living? What's she going to put on a job résumé? "Many years experience, wild-side walking"?

I've got other things to do with my life.

WHEN PIGS FLY
I WILL DO WHAT YOU WANT
WHEN RATS SING
I'LL BE YOUR EVERYTHING
YOU DON'T KNOW ME
YOU DON'T WANNA
IF YOU DID YOU'D RUN AWA

Friday
home, after school

Ms. Sevekow snuck up behind me while I was writing that. I had my journal onscreen too. I had to slam both my notebook and my laptop shut.

Ms. Sevekow made a big deal out of this. "MAGgie BLUME, could that POSsibly be YOU?" she said. As if I were some angel who'd just lost her wings.

Everyone laughed at me.

I have to be more careful in the future.

Okay, today's big news: The day was not a total washout.

I think I have a new friend. Maybe three.

Amalia Vargas is cool. I saw her as I was leaving school. I was alone, because Sunny had to run off somewhere and Dawn was still in school, in some deep conversation near the lockers with Ducky McCrae.

Amalia was with Cece deFarge and Marina Kodaly. I've never really known them well, but they were both giving me big smiles.

"Amalia told us you have a great voice," Marina said.

I could not believe Amalia had done that. My face must have turned three shades of red.

Well, we got to talking, and it turns out that Marina's brother is James, the guy Amalia likes. And all three girls are planning to go to Vanish's practice on Saturday night, in Rico Chavez's garage. And they invited me to come.

I smelled a rat. I told Amalia I was *not* going to sing.

"No one'll force you," she said. "Just hang out with us."

We stopped at the corner of Elliot Road. Since I had to go off in another direction, we stood there for awhile to talk.

And who should come walking toward us but Justin Randall.

Smiling.

"Hey," he said.

"Hey," replied Marina. "You coming Saturday?"

Justin shrugged and said okay.

As he walked away, I must have been staring, because Cece said, "Cute, huh?"

"I guess," I replied.

"He's free," Amalia said with a smile. "In case you're having any ideas."

Cece nudged me. "*Now* will you come to the rehearsal?"

Here's the weird thing: If Sunny had said something like that, I would have gotten angry.

But the way Amalia and Cece were talking, I couldn't.

And I had to admit something to myself.

I was relieved.

I mean, Justin Randall is nice-looking. And he might be fun to get to know. And I *know* he noticed me at that awful party at Ms. Krueger's, after I was thrown into the pool. Well, maybe he just noticed what was under my soaked shirt. But still.

Anyway, I said I'd check with Mom and Dad about Saturday night.

I'm sure I have nothing planned.

It just doesn't make sense.

Why doesn't Dad want me to go to the rehearsal?

He lets me go to rock concerts in other kids' cars. He once let me see *The Rocky Horror Picture Show* on a Saturday at midnight without a parent chaperone.

I know. This is all because of his focus group. 50 people saw a screening of *Fatal Judgment* and only 8 of them rated it "excellent." Which means the film has to go back to the editing room and some scenes may have to be reshot and the director is already shooting another film and the company's overbudget, etc., etc., etc.

Dad is frustrated. And so his first response to anything is no.

And Mom just goes along with him.

I'll have to work on her. Deep down, I know she really doesn't mind. She's just frustrated too. Pilar isn't answering her phone calls and Mom's desperate to hire her back.

It's Friday. VCR night. She rented *Hail the Conquering Hero.* Preston Sturges movies always put her in a good mood. I'll ask her again after we finish watching.

Friday
11:53 P.M.

Good news.

She said yes.

I told that to Dad when he called a few minutes ago. He'd forgotten I'd ever asked him at all.

So he agreed.

Thank you, Preston Sturges.

Saturday 11/15
12:01 P.M.

Amalia came over this morning. She is just great. Really down-to-earth.

She complimented me about the house, but she didn't go overboard. She didn't read all the autographed photos on the walls.

She even knows how to handle Zeke. When he first saw her, he asked me, "Who's the dork?"

She answered, "I was about to ask the same question." Somehow, within minutes they were laughing at each other's jokes.

I was impressed.

Anyway, she had a tape of Vanish and we listened to it.

I guess they're pretty good, for high school kids. It's hard to tell, though, because the backup singer is kind of dull (and way out of tune).

Was kind of dull. Amalia reminded me the singer had quit.

But she insists she will not make me sing. James is doing the backup vocals until they audition someone else.

The other headline of the day: Dad now thinks I should learn the cello. He knows someone who knows someone who taught the great cellist Yo Yo Ma. And Yo Yo Ma went to Harvard. This means a lot to Dad.

So, at the moment I'm listening to a Schubert cello sonata. But I'm thinking about rock tunes.

Amalia had to go home, but she's picking me up tonight.

After Schubert's over, I'll put on the Vanish tape again.

Saturday
sometime past midnight

How can I sleep? I am totally juiced up. It feels like noon.

Just got back from Rico's house. What an evening.

It started at 6:00. I was waiting for Amalia to pick me up, when a red Taurus rolled up our driveway. Amalia was waving at me from the front seat. Marina and Cece were in the back.

I figured it was the Vargas family car, but I was wrong. In the driver's seat, staring goggle-eyed at our house, was none other than Justin Randall.

As I climbed into the backseat, Zeke came to the front door. He shouted out, "Is that your boyfriend?"

Everyone in the car laughed. (I will kill him tomorrow.)

After what Sunny had said about Justin, I half expected him to ask all about Dad and the movie business. But he didn't. He just said, "Cool house," and that was that.

We listened to the Vanish tape all the way to Rico's. We could not stop talking. Amalia and Justin both know a lot about music. They had all kinds of suggestions about how to improve the group's sound.

Rico's house is in a pretty funky part of town that I don't know very well. As we got out of the car, Justin and I were in the middle of a conversation, so we walked across Rico's lawn together.

Justin is a really sweet guy. Funny too, and a lot smarter than I thought he was. Even though I shouldn't assume that someone isn't smart just because he looks the way Justin does, which is really really handsome.

We talked about Vanish. We talked about rock music in general. We talked about male singers versus female singers. We even talked about guitar fingerings (he takes lessons). I didn't want to stop talking.

The group was already tuning up in an enormous garage that had been converted into a performance/recording space. An older guy with a salt-and-pepper ponytail was adjusting sound levels, while a woman played keyboard riffs.

They introduced themselves as Rico's parents. I was amazed. They were so cool. Relaxed. They treated Rico as if he were a buddy, joking around and talking music. Then, after they finished setting up, they left. So unlike Mom and Dad.

Justin wandered off to talk to a couple of other high school guys, visitors like us. Amalia introduced me to James, Rico, and the other band members, Patti and Bruce. I liked them all.

As rehearsal began, Amalia, Cece, Marina, and I sat in folding chairs. James announced that the band's looking for a backup vocalist but he would fill in. He warned us not to laugh.

After a couple of songs, laughing wasn't the first thing that came to my mind. Cringing, maybe. James doesn't have much of a voice.

Which is too bad, because in person the band sounds even better than it does on tape.

Rico and James are fantastic guitarists (and Rico's not a bad lead vocalist), Patti drums like a pro, and Bruce's bass playing is solid.

On the third time through "Calico Rat Love Blues," James seemed to lose interest in the vocals and dropped out. Amalia, Marina, and Cece began singing along softly. I joined in too.

Rico looked our way and smiled. "Louder," he said.

We started wailing. The music was cranked up so high, we could barely hear ourselves.

At the first break, Rico's parents brought in doughnuts and soft drinks. As we all gathered around them, Justin smiled at me and said, "You have some set of pipes." (I didn't know what to make of that, but Amalia assures me that *set of pipes* is another way of saying *voice*.)

I couldn't believe he could hear me.

Well, he started urging me to try out for the band. I told him Amalia had already asked. He said, "She has good taste."

Right in the middle of our conversation, Patti, the drummer, walked up to Justin and started flirting. Heavily too. Putting her arms around his shoulders, feeding him hunks of doughnut, the works.

I just turned away.

Amalia caught my eye. She came toward me, smiling, but when she saw my face she grew really serious.

"Are you okay?" she asked.

"Sure," I replied. "Why?"

"You look upset."

I shrugged. "Nope. Fine."

But I *was* upset.

Upset at Patti for interrupting my conversation. Upset at Justin for turning away from me.

Upset at myself too.

For caring.

I did care. I cared that Justin was more interested in her than me. I cared that he liked my voice.

I cared about a guy who is at least three years older than me and wouldn't have the slightest interest in me.

He *should* go out with Patti. She's closer to his age.

Well, the flirtation didn't last long. The

band had to start up again. This time they played a ballad, "Fallen Angel." The notes were way out of Rico's range. And he's clearly much more comfortable singing fast songs.

Marina nudged me. "You should go up there."

I shook my head. But as I sat there, my legs felt all twitchy. Part of me wanted to run up and grab the mike. I could definitely sing it better than Rico.

I stayed put, though. I'm not crazy.

Besides, I wouldn't feel comfortable singing those words. The lyrics need work. Too many bad rhymes.

At around 11:00, the rehearsal broke up. James looked depressed. He told Amalia the group needs at least another couple of rehearsals this week.

"What's the use of rehearsing if we don't have a backup vocalist?" Rico asked.

"We'll get one," James insisted.

"In time for the Battle of the Bands?" Rico said.

Amalia volunteered to post an audition notice on-line. I said I'd type up a flyer to put around the school.

We all kept reassuring the band how good the rehearsal was, but they didn't believe us. Their good-byes were kind of glum.

On the way home, the car was pretty quiet. Justin didn't put on a tape or the radio. I think we were music-ed out.

I had the weirdest feeling. Kind of empty and achy and sad.

I'm not sure why.

Dad's home. Just heard him come in the front door.

I didn't realize he was out. I thought he was home sleeping.

Midnight on a Saturday? This film must be in big trouble.

More tomorrow.

technically Sunday 11/16
1:15 A.M.

I didn't shut my light in time.

Dad came stomping upstairs, demanding to know why I was still awake. Then he demanded to know what time I came home.

Then he demanded to know where I'd been —
even though I'd already told him.

When I reminded him, he blew up.

"You were out till midnight listening to
a *garage band*?" he said.

I could have gone to "a great
Philharmonic concert." He could have gotten
me tickets to a touring company of a
Broadway show. Or I could have used the
time practicing piano.

What I want to know is, *Why didn't he
bring this up when I first asked?*

He is totally irrational. I cannot wait for
the premiere, so he'll become normal again.

Sunday 11/16
11:32 A.M.

Had a dream last night. I was in the
army, returning to Palo City during wartime.
I hadn't even served, but everyone was
greeting me as if I were some great hero —
parades and awards, commemorative
statues, everything — just like the guy in
Hail the Conquering Hero. In my dream, Justin

had stayed home from the war for some reason. We were in love, and he found out about my lie. But he didn't mind a bit. We were about to kiss when I woke up.

I must admit, this means *something.*

This is not healthy. Unrequited love is bad for the soul. Everyone knows that. I have to get over it somehow.

Thank goodness Amalia called this morning. I blurted out all my complaints about Dad. She added a few choice ones about her dad. We were howling with laughter after a few minutes.

Then we talked about last night's rehearsal. I mentioned how strange I felt in the car.

Amalia's first reaction was, "You really like him, huh?"

"Who?" I asked.

"Justin. Who else?"

Just like that. I hadn't even given the slightest opinion of him.

"Was I that obvious?" I said.

Amalia laughed. "I don't think so. I just know you, that's all."

"But we haven't been friends that long."

"I know. It feels as if we have, though. Isn't that weird?"

It is weird. But a good kind of weird. I feel as if Amalia is some kind of long-lost sister. She's so open and smart. The kind of person I can talk to about anything.

So I tried to explain how I felt about Justin. It wasn't easy. Mainly because I'm not totally sure myself.

When I asked her what I should do, she sighed deeply. It turned out that she feels just as confused about James. They hang together at school and sometimes go out, but they've never kissed or anything. "The right occasion just hasn't happened," she said. "Besides, I keep thinking he might like Patti."

I knew what that felt like.

We decided boys are a total mystery and not worth it.

Maybe.

Next topic: Vanish auditions. Amalia said the group wanted to have them on Thursday. James had decided he would teach each auditioner two songs: "Hook Shot" and "Fallen Angel."

"Maybe not 'Fallen Angel,'" I said. "We want the auditioners to *like* the music."

Amalia laughed. "I know what you mean. So why don't you rewrite it?"

"No way," I replied. "I don't want to insult them."

"They'd fall on their knees and kiss your feet," Amalia replied, "if they knew what was good for them."

She is so flattering.

After we hung up, I prepared a flyer. Simple and direct. It looks like this:

!! FEMALE **BACKUP SINGER** NEEDED !!
FOR PALO CITY'S
NUMBER-ONE ROCK BAND
VANISH
MUST SING POP, R&B, ROCK
AUDITION ON THURSDAY NOVEMBER 20 — 7 PM
RICO CHAVEZ'S GARAGE
1371 PALOMITO AVE.

On neon-colored paper, it'll look great.

FALLEN ANGEL — new lyrics
Respectfully suggested by Maggie Blume

Down to earth,
Feet on the ground,
I look straight ahead
Don't turn around.
In all I do,
I'm here for you.
I'm your Fallen Angel.

Stretch my arms,
Reach to the sky,
My wings are broken
But I need to fly.
Look at me,
I'm not what you see,
I'm a Fallen Angel.
Fly high
Where the eagle sings
Fly high
Fix these broken wings

A breath of wind
A whisper of sound

I rise through the mist
With my feet off the ground
Won't you come with me?
'cause I don't want to be
A Fallen Angel
A Fallen Angel.

© Maggie Blume

Sunday 11/16
8:07 P.M.

I can't show this to James.

It wouldn't be right. It would be like saying, *I'm better than you.*

But I do like it a lot more than his version.

Oh, well. I can always give it a different title and print it in *Inner Vistas.* I am the poetry editor, after all.

Monday 11/17
9:05 P.M.

I'm fastening my seat belt.

The teachers are piling on the work. They

see the end of the marking period coming, and they realize they haven't gone as fast as they were supposed to.

So we students have to suffer.

Just what I need.

Couldn't write in this journal at all today. Too much work. Can't write much now either. Math *and* English exams tomorrow.

So just a quick recap for now.

Morning. I put up Vanish flyers all over Vista.

Lunch. Sunny and Dawn sat by themselves in a corner. Sunny looked like she was crying. I asked Dawn about it later. She said Sunny's been staying at the Schafers' a lot. Sunny still feels so trapped by all the painful happenings in her life. Sometimes she wants to run away again, even though her last attempt was very scary.

Just out of curiosity, I asked if Sunny seemed at all interested in Justin. Dawn looked at me as if I were crazy. "After what happened at Venice Beach, Sunny's sworn off boys for awhile," she said.

I feel guilty for judging Sunny. I've got to apologize.

After school. On the way to the *Inner Vistas* meeting, I saw at least a dozen kids reading the audition flyer in the front hall.

At the meeting, I showed "Fallen Angel" to Parker Price. (I told her it was a poem.) She read it carefully, then murmured, "Verse, verse, bridge, verse. It sounds like song lyrics."

How did she get so smart?

Home. Study. Practice Beethoven. Study. Play with the cats. Study.

I am beat.

I cannot look at one more textbook.

But I have this idea for a poem. Just fragments and thoughts.

For Sunny
We held hands at the Hollywood Bowl
As the summer sun set
I was afraid I'd be lost
If I let go.
We were two, we were three,
We were thirteen.
And still the sun sets
But my fingers grip air
And I feel lost.

Have I let go
Or have you?
Rise, my friend,
Blaze, my friend.
Use your light
And find me, my friend.

Tuesday 11/18
5:05 P.M.

I have flunked.

I could not keep my eyes open during the math exam.

I was so flustered, I went on to botch the English test. I had to race through the last two essay questions.

I almost cried on the way home.

Why should I even bother going to school tomorrow to get my grades? I know what they'll be. F and F.

The last person I wanted to see today was Mrs. Knudsen. When she showed up, I was feeling so depressed. I almost asked her to go home.

It was my worst lesson ever. Mrs.

Knudsen actually stopped me at one point and asked if I needed something to eat. "You seem a bit fragile," was how she put it.

Fragile was exactly the right word. I could feel myself starting to cry.

She was looking at me so patiently. Forgivingly. As if the Beethoven didn't matter as much as I did.

So I told her how I was feeling. About the tests today. The tension in the house. My worries about the future. Then I blurted out, "The only thing that gives me any pleasure is my writing."

That was stupid. As soon as the words left my mouth, I realized I was insulting her. Like I hated my lessons.

Mrs. Knudsen was giving me this hurt look. I tried to cover up. I said I liked music too — but since I believe it is *connected* to writing, I hadn't mentioned music specifically.

Mrs. Knudsen's face suddenly brightened. She asked if I'd been composing, and could I show her my "pieces."

That was when I should have shut my big mouth. "You wouldn't like them," I said.

"They're rock songs. I wrote one for this group that I'm thinking of joining. As a singer/songwriter."

I nearly melted into the piano bench. I mean, I haven't admitted that to *anybody.*

Mrs. Knudsen nodded. "When I was a little older than you, I ran away from home to sing in a big band. I was going to be the next Anita Oday or Rosemary Cloony." [Something like that.] "I was just as good as they were. Better."

"Ran away? *You?*" I was shocked.

"I wasn't gone long. The band broke up and I returned home. But I never lost my love for music. It just grew in a different direction."

"Are you glad you did it?"

"Well, my parents never did forgive me. I feel as though I lost their trust." Mrs. Knudsen placed her hand gently on mine. "Think about this carefully, Maggie. Experiment, yes. That's what youth is for. But measure the pros and cons, and don't let yourself get in so far that it takes over your life. And definitely avoid burning your bridges. Your parents love you, even though that may be hard to see."

How utterly strange.

When I try to imagine Mrs. Knudsen as a runaway band singer, I picture a white-haired lady with spectacles and a leather jacket, smoking a cigarette and riding a motorbike.

But it's nice to know she was a normal kid. She liked the pop music of her time. And she actually did something I'm too chicken to do myself.

So . . . what if I do take her advice?

JOINING VANISH — PROS AND CONS

CONS:
I would:
1. Not have enough time for homework and *Inner Vistas* duties.
2. Possibly flunk school.
3. Be involved in something that has no impact on my future whatsoever.
4. Totally give up on finding another extracurricular activity.

5. Have to buy new wardrobe.
6. Get a reputation I don't want. (Like what's happening to Sunny.)
7. Lose sleep.
8. Make Mom and Dad angry.

PROS:
I would:
1. Find out if I really can sing.
2. Find out how good my songwriting really is.
3. Do something *I* want to do.
4. Have fun.
5. Hang out with kids I like.
6. Possibly get to know Justin.
7. Get out of the house more often.
8. Make Mom and Dad angry.
   Eight to eight. Not such a big help.
   Oh, well. Maybe by Thursday night it'll all be a moot point. Vanish will find some fantastic singer, 10 times better than me, and I'll be off the hook.
   I have to forget about it. IN THE LONG RUN, IT IS NOT IMPORTANT.

There's a war. Inside.
In the battlefield of my brain.
Should I stand and fight?
Or will it drive me insane?
I'm a rebel. You don't like it?
Then just get out of my way.
You tell me you're the future.
Well, the future's far away.
This is now.
This is me.
This is War.
I can feel you all around me.
All righteous. Not a doubt.
Well, time to choose a weapon.
'cause now I'm coming out.
Raise my head above the muck.
Take my aim, you're out of luck.
But I drop my gun and duck.
'cause the enemy
The face I see
Is me.

A 101 on my math exam.

English, 97.

I'm still in shock.

I did not want to make a big deal about the grades, but Dawn asked point-blank at the lunch table. So I had to announce them in front of her, Sunny, Amalia, Marina, and Cece.

Dawn laughed at me. She said maybe I hadn't worried enough. If I had, I might have gotten a 101 on the English too.

"Look, if I didn't worry, my grades wouldn't be so good," I explained.

Sunny groaned. "Yeah, your average might drop to a 97."

"You'd be a lot happier," Amalia suggested.

"I *am* happy," I protested. "I just want to do well in school. Don't you?"

"If I had your brains, your work habits, and your talent," Amalia said, "I wouldn't be worried a bit."

"I'd be singing in *two* bands," Sunny added.

I told them all that they didn't understand. That they should try being in my shoes.

Amalia said that I should step *out* of my shoes. I should pretend to be someone else looking at me. Make it into an exercise.

I know she meant well, but I felt picked on. So I clammed up and ate.

But I thought and thought about it. And I tried out that exercise. Just a few minutes ago.

Stepping out of myself is easy. In a way, I do that whenever I'm writing.

But I don't look at myself when I write. I look out. At the world.

So just now I pretended that I was a fly, hiding just inside the overhead fluorescent light. And I imagined looking down.

I scanned the room, looking at all the kids.

But when I got to myself, I had the most horrible feeling.

A huge inferiority complex.

I saw the money. The nice clothes. The house and the pool. The grades.

Then I suddenly wanted to cry. Because I could see my face. It was so tight and sad.

And I had this image of an invisible cage around me.

Then I started hearing my song lyrics. And *that's* when I stopped the exercise.

I was convincing myself I was one of the characters in my songs. Which is just not true.

Those lyrics are *not* about *me.*

I just write them. They pour out.

They're just songs.

Wednesday night

Hey
Down There
Who are you?
Why do you look at me the way you do?
Eyes
like leather
Aged and tough
Won't let me in; they say you've had enough.

Well, you write and you write, and your words just lock
   you in.
And sooner or later they'll harden like a second skin.
Open up.
Unlock the gate.
You're young enough
To control your fate.
Do it now.
Before it's too late.
Hey
Down there.
I love you.

© Maggie Blume

11/20

   I just looked over my list of pros and
cons. I decided most of the cons are
ridiculous.
   Back when Amalia asked me to sing with
the band, I should have said yes.
   If I had, there would be no audition now.
I would be Vanish's official backup singer.
Dad would be annoyed, but he'd get over it.
I'd find time to study and edit poems.

Now it's too late. Tonight's the audition. In a few hours, some future Madonna is going to show up in Rico's garage.

I have really, really blown it.

Thursday
11:31 P.M.

Right now, I do not know how to feel.

I am ecstatic.

I am angry.

I am confused.

At dinner tonight, I could not eat a thing. Mom had ordered a fancy meal with all these heavy sauces from some French restaurant. Zeke kept making gagging noises and demanded we go out to Wendy's. By the end of the meal, Mom was pretty disgusted with both of us.

Normally I wouldn't have minded eating, but all I could think about was the audition. I'd told Amalia I'd go help out, but the thought of watching all the singers was making me sick.

This time Rico's dad picked me up, not

Justin. I was relieved. I didn't need one more thing making me nervous.

About 10 girls were gathered outside Rico's garage door. They all looked *perfect.* Like they just stepped out of a music video. Weird hair, body jewelry, cool sunglasses, clothes never before seen on a human. As Amalia and I walked toward the garage, I felt so conspicuous in my chinos, Topsiders, polo shirt, and headband. The auditioners were all giving me these what-is-*she*-doing-here? looks. If they looked at me at all.

Good old Amalia didn't seem fazed a bit. I followed her inside and tried to absorb her attitude.

Marina was there too. Her job was to let the girls in one by one.

The first girl's name was Amethyst. She was absolutely gorgeous. Her outfit was so incredibly revealing that the guys could not stop staring at her. Amalia and I were cracking up. But the moment she opened her mouth, no one was amused. She sounded like a screaming tomcat.

The next girl had a good voice but

couldn't find the right key. She kept stopping the audition and asking the band members to tune up.

Number three was okay too, but she was a professional actress and she demanded that James contact her agent to discuss her "share of any future recording profits."

At first, Amalia and I tried hard to clap for everyone and look encouraging. James would thank each girl and promise to call back.

Then he would turn to us and make a face.

By the end, 19 girls had auditioned. Only five of them were good. And three of those were great. At least I thought so.

Not James. He looked completely depressed by the time the last girl left. He practically threw his guitar on the floor in disgust. "I'm calling Backstreet and canceling," he said, stomping off.

Amalia ran after him.

Rico, Patti, and Bruce were listlessly unhooking their wires.

Marina suggested they have another audition later in the week. Rico said the

Battle of the Bands was only 12 days away, and it would be hard to get someone to learn all the music by then.

I mentioned the names of the three girls I liked.

"I hated them," Rico replied flatly. "They don't fit with the group."

Patti gave me kind of a weary half smile. "*You* should have auditioned."

"She's great," Marina blurted out.

"Yeah?" Rico picked up his guitar again. "Can you do the harmonies on 'Hook Shot'?"

I froze up. I could not get my mouth to work.

"Sure she can," Marina said. "I'll get James!"

She raced out of the garage.

I wanted to follow her, but I couldn't move. I was petrified.

Then Bruce started playing the bass line.

Patti came in with a strong beat.

Rico grabbed his guitar and called out, "One . . . two . . . three . . . four!"

He launched into the song himself.

I was stuck.

I opened my mouth and squawked. That is

the best way I can describe the sound that came out.

Rico gestured toward James's mike.

I unlocked my knees and walked toward it. Patti and Bruce were beaming at me, nodding encouragingly.

I don't know how, but smack in the middle of the verse, I managed to find the harmony. It just came out of my mouth. Very softly. I could barely hear myself.

I moved closer to the mike. Now I could hear my voice blasting out of the monitors. I didn't *want* to be loud, but I had to be. It was the only way I could tell whether or not I was in tune.

It was the strangest sensation. I didn't feel as if I were performing. I didn't feel stage fright or fluttery stomach or anything.

I felt as if I were *working,* actually. Like taking a hard English exam.

When it was over, I was startled by a blast of raucous noise from the garage door.

It was James and Amalia, whistling and clapping and whooping at the top of their lungs. I'd been concentrating so hard I hadn't noticed them entering.

Before I could react, Rico had taken me by the shoulders. "Why didn't you *tell* us you could do this?" he exclaimed. "We wouldn't have had to listen to all those turkeys."

I didn't even answer. All I could do was grin.

I felt Amalia's and Marina's arms around me. And I heard James say, "You're in. Let's start rehearsing now."

So we did.

I, Maggie Blume, am now the backup singer for Vanish.

It feels so good to write that.

I learned the backup vocals for three songs. I learned how to play the tambourine.

Everyone was so encouraging. They asked me to come to the next rehearsal, on Saturday. And maybe —just maybe —I'll learn enough guitar to join in.

I had so much fun, I'm still shaking.

Nothing could make me come down. Not even what happened when I got home.

Dad was at the front door, watching, as Mr. Chavez dropped me off. He glared at me while I walked toward the front door.

"It's almost midnight," were his first words.

I didn't care how angry he was. I was excited enough for at least three people. I threw my arms around him and gave him a big kiss.

"I'm in —" I began. I was going to say Vanish. But I stopped myself. I could tell Dad wasn't ready to hear this news quite yet.

"In what?" he grumbled. "In *love*? Don't tell me . . ."

I laughed and said something ridiculous like "in with a new group of friends." Then I went straight into the kitchen. I was starving.

Mom was sitting there in her silk bathrobe, over a cup of decaf and a stack of papers. She watched me warily over her reading glasses. "Tomorrow's a school day," she reminded me.

"I know," I said.

Dad was pacing the kitchen now, barking into his cell phone. "What do you mean, the house manager has rented the theater? *Un*rent it! Where are we supposed to have the premiere, in the YMCA?"

I looked at Mom. She smiled and rolled her eyes.

Dad slammed the phone down. "Now — *now* they find this out. We've got the caterers lined up for the party, the spotlights are rented . . ." etc., etc., etc.

I listened with half an ear. That's the only way I can deal with Dad when he's like this.

Sometimes I wish he were more like Dawn's father. He *never* talks about work when he's home.

Then I think, Dad wouldn't have gotten where he is today without being so obsessed. The fates of major films ride on his shoulders. It's such an awesome job. And he still manages to be a good father (providing it's not too close to premiere dates).

"They have the nerve to ask if I can change the date!" Dad was thundering. "I told them it's *their* problem now. The media will be at the theater door at 6:00 on December 2nd, expecting a premiere! We have the main dining room of Duomo rented for the party — next door! Which reminds me. You do have something nice to wear to the party, don't you, Maggie?"

I told Dad I'd check my closet.

On the way to my room, I had a funny feeling.

Inside, I shut the door behind me and quickly tapped out Amalia's number.

She answered the line in a hushed voice. Her parents were asleep. (Lucky her.)

"Amalia, when's the Battle of the Bands?"

"A week from Tuesday. The first band goes on at 6:45, I think."

"I mean, what's the *date*?"

"I think it's December 2nd. Why?"

"*The 2nd?* That's the premiere of *Fatal Judgment*!"

"So?"

"So I have to go! My dad's the producer!"

"Tell him you have something else to do. *You're* not the producer."

"It's not that easy, Amalia."

"Well, sleep on it, okay? Don't jump to any rash decisions."

Some people just can't understand.

I am sunk.

Dead in the water.

I have had a whole night to think about my dilemma.

During most of it, I was wide awake. My mind was like a twister.

First of all, I could not erase the image of those three auditioners. They were *much* better singers than me. And they *looked* the part too.

I mean, what exactly did I do that was so great? I went up there dressed like Nancy Drew. I blasted harmonies at the top of my lungs, without a smile, staring at the mike.

And they want *me* to be the backup singer?

What is wrong with this picture?

I keep thinking of the last Drama Club play I did, last year. When Mr. Colker asked me to play the lead in *Mame* even though I'd signed up for stage crew. I was so flattered — until Polly Guest overheard Mr. Colker say to someone over the phone, "I just cast Hayden Blume's daughter as the lead. Maybe I can write my ticket out of this job after all."

He was using me. He thought that by casting me, he'd meet Dad, and Dad would make him a star director. Or whatever it was that Mr. Colker wanted to be.

I am so glad I turned that down. When I mentioned the situation to Dad, he said, "Unfortunately, you'll always have to be looking out for that sort of thing, sweetheart."

So I do.

And I'm thinking, *Is that what's happening here?*

James and Rico know who Dad is. They must know he's pals with all the record company executives.

Is that why they just happened to pick me over those other girls?

But Amalia insists that I'm good. I don't think she'd lie.

And I can do harmonies. That's what backup singers do. So maybe I'm wrong. Maybe the other singers were *too* strong — soloists, really. Maybe James and Rico need someone who will blend in, not steal focus. I'm great at that.

This is all so confusing.

Okay, let's say they are being honest. They like me. Now what? How can I agree to join them? I can't be in two places at once on December 2nd. Period.

I have to quit Vanish. That's all there is to it.

The sooner I do it, the less painful it'll be. I've only been a member for half a day.

I will call Amalia and tell her right now.

Friday
4:17 P.M.

My head is spinning.

This morning when I told Amalia I'd quit, and I mentioned my suspicions, she practically yelled at me.

"These guys aren't thinking of *record contracts*," she said. "They're sophomores and juniors! Look, Maggie, you have to have more self-confidence. You do great vocals."

Then I reminded her about my conflict with the movie premiere.

"That's a different story," she said. "Have you discussed this with your dad?"

I told her I couldn't. In his frame of mind, he wouldn't understand.

"Maybe he would *like* the idea," Amalia suggested. "I mean, he's your father. He cares about you."

Patiently I explained how important premieres are. How Dad can't be bothered by trivial things until the opening weekend grosses are in.

"Trivial?" Amalia asked. "Is that *you* talking or him?"

That really stopped me. Like a slap in the face. "Me, of course," I snapped.

"I have to be honest," Amalia said. "It sounds like you're doing what *he* wants. Not even that — what you *think* he wants. What about *you,* Maggie? Do you really want to quit Vanish?"

I told her the truth: no.

Amalia told me not to rush things. To pretend our conversation hadn't happened. She promised not to tell James I quit.

"But what am I going to do?" I asked.

"Whenever I have to make a big decision, I talk it out with *all* my friends. I take a poll. And I listen to everyone's advice. Eventually the answer becomes clear."

That made sense. I agreed to give it a try.

Before homeroom, at our lockers, I told Dawn what had happened.

She disagreed with Amalia.

"You're not quitting for your dad," she said. "You're doing it for your family. To be with them on an important night. There's nothing wrong with that."

I hadn't really thought of it that way.

One for the "quit" column.

I was going to ask Sunny at lunch. But I still felt so much tension between us. So I ended up apologizing to her. I told her I shouldn't have been so cold and judgmental.

Then I reached into my pack and gave her a copy of the poem I wrote to her.

She read it carefully. She looked as if she wanted to cry, but she covered it with giggles and told me I was "talented."

Anyway, I did have a chance to tell her

about *my* problem, after school. (I told Ducky too, but only because he happened to be hanging out with her.)

"Don't you dare drop out," Sunny said.

When I asked why, she began counting on her fingers: "One. You are the smartest and most talented person I know — even though I hate your wardrobe — and you should *explore* those talents. Two. Your father has premieres all the time, but the Battle of the Bands happens once a year. Three. If you don't go, maybe I can go in your place." She grinned. "Huh? Could I?"

Ducky groaned. I couldn't help smiling myself.

"Maybe you can compromise," Ducky said. "Tell me a little about your dad's party."

I described a premiere. The dull screening, at which everyone watches a movie they've all seen before. The reception at which Dad plays big shot, introduces his family all around, and tries to drum up money for his next film.

"There you go," Ducky said. "Skip the boring movie. Go to the Battle of the Bands first, then catch your family later at the party."

"How?" I asked. "Backstreet is in Palo City and the party's in Beverly Hills."

"I'll drive you," Ducky volunteered.

"Pick me up on the way!" Sunny said.

(She was joking. I hope.)

Anyway, Ducky's solution sounds perfect. He is such a good guy. When Dad comes home tonight — *if* Dad comes home — I'll bring it up.

Friday
7:52 P.M.

Less talk
More killing.
More tickets.
Less fulfilling.
Cut the words.
Cut off some limbs.
Count the money
Then do it again.
This is your life, Dad
Cash on a platter.

Are you proud of yourself
For making it matter?
When I stand by your side
Tell me, who do you see?
Am I your mirror
Or am I me?
How are my wishes
Worse than yours?
Must I be with you
On all of your chores?
I'm a beast of burden
Not a bird that soars
And the sound that I hear
Is the closing of doors.

Friday
9:17 P.M.

I asked him politely.

I was very reasonable.

I waited until he finished his dinner and looked relaxed.

I had scripted exactly what I needed to tell him, and I stuck to it word for word.

And I remember our conversation word for word, as if it were a screenplay.

"Dad," I said, "I really want to go to the opening night party. I know how important that is. And I also know that we've seen *Fatal Judgment* already, so the screening is kind of a formality."

Dad chuckled at that. "I'll say. Hit me if I fall asleep before the second reel."

"So, my friend Ducky has agreed to drive me to the party so I don't miss one minute of it," I went on. "Isn't that great?"

Dad gave me a blank look. "Why would you need a ride? Aren't you coming with us?"

"Well, I was sort of hoping, since it doesn't matter if I miss the screening, that I could go to this club called Backstreet. They're having a Battle of the Bands, and some high school bands are competing for a prize, so it's very important."

"Really? Is this Ducky fellow in one of the groups?" Dad asked.

I braced myself. "Well, no. *I* am."

"Cool!" Zeke exclaimed.

Dad sat forward. "Wait. This is the group whose audition you went to see the other night? At Chico's house?"

"Rico's."

"You didn't tell us *you* were auditioning," Mom said.

"I didn't intend to audition," I explained. "But they didn't like any of the other singers, so they made me try, and . . . I got it."

I was so wrong about Dad's mood.

He was not relaxed.

He was like a time bomb.

He literally shot up from the chair. His face was red. "*This* is the after-school activity you get involved in? *A garage band?*"

"They're good musicians," I insisted. "Practically professional."

"*Beethoven* was a good musician. Bach. Brahms."

"But they're dead."

"You want to meet a good, *live* musician? Fine. I'll call Bill Johns tomorrow. He scored my last movie. One hour with him, and you'll learn so much about music your head'll spin."

"But that's a different kind of music —" I protested.

"Trust me, Maggie, scratch the surface of any popular musician today — pop, jazz, even the best rock performers — and what do you find? Classical training! Hours of practice as a child."

"Dad, I'm not a child," I said.

"*You're 13!* Don't fool yourself. This isn't the Beatles here. It isn't the Philharmonic. These are kids mucking around on guitars. I know it seems glamorous, but don't be tempted by easy entertainment at your age. You have to be serious."

"*You* do easy entertainment, Dad. What's *Fatal Judgment*?"

"That's different! I make those so the studio can finance the more artistic movies. That's my job. But even to make action movies I had to pay my dues. I had to achieve. You know that, Maggie."

"I achieve too. I have a 98 average in school. I play piano. I'm in the Honor Society, *Inner Vistas.* That's a lot. I need to have fun too."

"So have fun! Invite your friends over! We have a video library of 2,000 titles. Today you call this group 'fun.' But already look what it's doing. You come home late on school nights. You want to skip out of a screening. What next?"

I was so angry and sad and shocked, I could barely speak. I fought back tears. Zeke had shot away and was rooting around in the fridge.

Mom was giving me a mournful look. "Your father's right," she said.

"My father's always right," I managed to mumble before I ran to my room.

Friday
10:51 P.M.

Just apologized to Dad.

He apologized back. He said he'd come down too hard.

Then he admitted something I never knew. He said he hates making blockbuster movies. He'd rather be making risky, interesting, low-budget films. Years ago his dream was to be a director/screenwriter, not a producer. But he didn't try hard enough in film school. The students who worked harder than he did, the ones who took their studies seriously and made "gutsy" films — *they're* the ones making the movies Dad wished he could make.

"Please understand, I'm just thinking of what's best for you, Maggie," he said.

It must have been hard for Dad to admit all that. I guess I was seeing him in a new light.

He wants to be the best, but he knows he's not. He works hard and assumes the worst is going to happen. He gets totally frantic when things go wrong.

None of which makes him easy to live with.

"I guess I understand," I told him. "But —"

Dad smiled and stood up. "I knew you'd come around. Maybe your friend can make a video of the Battle of the Bands. And if you really love singing rock songs, you and I can go shopping for some karaoke tapes after the premiere, okay?"

My stomach sank.

Here I was, going overboard to understand him, and he'd totally misread me. Interrupted me too.

As he walked out, I just said, "Sure, Dad."

And I meant it.

If he wants to buy me karaoke tapes, fine.

I did *not* say I'd go to the screening.

Friday
11:03 P.M.

Am I nuts?

Who am I trying to kid?

He's my father.

He's been there for me my whole life.

Okay, he has a temper. He gets a little crazy. But he's human and he cares about me.

He expects me to go.

I should go.

Besides, I told him, "Sure."

I can't just turn my back.

Why is my life so difficult?

Saturday, 11/22
8:37 P.M.

This morning James called. He wanted to change the rehearsal time from 1:00 to 2:00.

I knew just what to say. I formed the words in my head: *James, I have to quit.*

"James," I began.

I couldn't do it.

Not over the phone. It was too impersonal.

I had to tell the group face-to-face. As painful as it might be.

So I said okay.

Which meant I had the whole morning to worry.

"Hey, how are the golden pipes?" James asked as I walked in.

"Fine," I replied absently.

But I was thinking about Dad. About how I'd given him a compromise. About how I'd arranged to be at the party AND do what I wanted to do.

About how I'd been reasonable, and he'd said no.

And I came to the conclusion that he simply does not want me to have a life.

"Okay, let's set up!" Rico was calling out. "We don't have all day!"

The words I needed to say — "I quit" — were sliding further and further back into my mind.

I sang through "Hook Shot." I learned a couple of other tunes that we ran through about 10 times each.

James is an incredibly tough boss. We didn't break for almost two hours. My throat felt like raw hamburger.

Finally Mr. Chavez brought out some snacks and drinks.

As Amalia and I ate and chatted, James and Rico were heatedly talking about "Fallen Angel."

Rico was convinced Vanish should use it in the set at Backstreet. James was gently trying to tell him that the lyrics weren't good enough.

Amalia nudged me. "Didn't *you* write lyrics?" she asked.

"Yes," I said quietly, "but don't —"

Amalia turned to James and said, "Try Maggie's words."

I felt like melting into the floor. I was mortified. I mean, I barely knew Rico and I was already changing his song.

James asked me to write out my version. My hands were shaking when I did it.

Now I knew I wouldn't have to quit.

I'd be fired.

I was too nervous to stand around while James, Rico, Bruce, and Patti read the sheet. I wandered over to the keyboard and started playing softly.

I played around with the chords for "Hey, Down There," trying to fix the bridge. Of course, to do that, I had to sing along.

I guess I must have been concentrating hard. Because I made it all the way to the end of the song without stopping. And when I reached it, I realized I wasn't singing softly anymore.

I also realized no one had said a word to me the whole time.

They were all standing around the keyboard, staring at me.

Suddenly I felt clammy and nervous. I stood up quickly and apologized for playing on and on.

"It's okay," Rico mumbled.

He was giving me this strange look. They *all* were, even Amalia.

"I know, I shouldn't have changed the words," I said. "I wasn't going to show you."

"Words?" James asked.

"To 'Fallen Angel,'" I reminded him.

"We love those words," Rico said. "They're a hundred times better than mine. But what was that song you just played?"

"Just one of mine," I replied. "It's nothing."

Amalia shook her head. "It's not nothing," she said softly.

James asked me if I would mind playing it again.

Anything was better than standing there with my hands dangling. I sat back down and played the intro.

As I began the verse, I heard a gentle, steady beat. I glanced over and saw Patti at the drum set.

Bruce was setting up too, and he joined in with a low, thumping bass line.

Soon James and Rico were strumming guitars.

Suddenly "Hey, Down There" was a song.

My words, my melody — they sounded so *real.*

When we reached the last verse, I sat back and closed my eyes. I tried not to think about how my voice sounded. I just thought about the words and what they meant to me.

As the final chord faded into silence, I could see Amalia standing by the garage door with Mr. Chavez.

No one said anything for awhile.

James was the first to speak. "You know," he said, "we were wrong to make you our backup singer."

I swallowed hard. This was it. I knew it. They'd been humoring me. Letting me play my stupid composition before letting me go. "I'm —"

Sorry, I was about to say. But James cut me off. "We should have made you our *lead* singer."

"Amen," Mr. Chavez called out. "No offense, Rico."

Rico was beaming. "Does this mean I don't have to do vocals anymore?"

I wanted to scream.

I wanted to dance on the keyboard.

I wanted to lift up everyone and fly around the garage together.

But I'm me.

I just said thank you and had another snack.

One thing I did not do was quit.

I just couldn't.

Not after one of the happiest moments of my life.

Saturday

I just met
A great girl
I want you all to know.
You may not
Recognize her
So just say hello.
She's dancing

On starlight.
She's spinning round and round.
Please don't try
To catch her,
Her feet can't touch the ground.
Just put on
Dark glasses.
You'll need them for awhile.
Don't try to
Remove them;
She'll blind you with her smile.
Come closer,
I'll tell you
Just who this is about.
I'll bet you
Have guessed it.
As if there were a doubt.

© Maggie Blume

Saturday
10:03 P.M.

    I will never, ever show that song to another soul.

    It's conceited.

It's self-centered.
It's foolish.
It's exactly how I feel.

Sunday 11/23
10:11 A.M.

I've done it.

This is brilliant.

I just talked to Ducky on the phone. I hardly know him, but he seems okay. Sort of *on* all the time, but you get used to that. He has a great sense of humor. Anyway, he and I came up with a perfect plan.

I will go to the premiere with Mom and Dad. Before the screening begins, I will mix with the people in the theater hallway.

Then, just when the place is at its most jam-packed, I will sneak out. Ducky will be waiting for me in the getaway car. We will zip over to Backstreet in time for the Battle of the Bands. Then, after Vanish's turn, Ducky will drive me back in time for the party.

I love it.

It's like something out of one of Dad's films.

I was so excited about my plan today, I forgot one major missing ingredient.

I realized this when Mom took me and Zeke into Beverly Hills today. We went shopping on Rodeo Drive, supposedly for outfits for the premiere. Mom's personal shopper at Federico Boutique found her this long gold lamé gown with dropped shoulders. Then Mom made me try on some outfits. Every single one made me look about 40 years old.

I was wearing some frilly thing, staring at myself in the mirror, when it hit me.

I needed a Look.

A real, thought-out Look. Not just ordinary, everyday Maggie-wear.

Punk. Grunge. Retro. *Something.*

I quickly changed back into my street clothes. I told Mom not to buy me a new outfit. I'd wear something I had in my closet. Zeke was bored and cranky. He said he'd go in his underwear.

Finally he wore Mom down. On our way to the car we passed by this new clothing store that had all kinds of funky outfits in the window. Mom kind of sniffed and said, "I am *so* glad you don't dress like that anymore."

But I did see something I liked a lot. It was a seventies-style tight striped rayon dress. Very retro and very cool.

I asked Mom about it. She just gave me the eye and said, "Maggie, don't make trouble."

Oh, well. I couldn't wear it anyway. I am way too fat.

Tomorrow I'll start my diet.

Monday 11/24
10:09 P.M.

Can't write much. Tired. Tons of homework. Social studies test tomorrow. I will not say I'm going to flunk it.

I will not worry.

What have I gotten myself into?

I was wrong last night.

I *should* have worried.

A lot.

My test was awful. A nightmare. I don't even want to write about it.

Everything Dad said about joining a rock band is true.

It is taking over my life. Today, before homeroom, James appeared at my locker to tell me about our next rehearsal. This afternoon.

At the same time as my piano lesson.

Did I put my foot down? Did I tell James I had to play a Beethoven sonata for Olivia Knudsen?

No. I mumbled something about a prior family commitment.

Dawn was giving me her best *honesty-is-the-best-policy* look. Sunny was staring at James, her jaw practically scraping the ground, as if he were an Elvis sighting.

Ducky, who was hanging out with us, just looked confused.

"Can you come late at least?" James asked.

"Uh, um, uh," I replied.

"I can drive you," Ducky volunteered.

Later on, that is exactly what he did (after a dreadful piano lesson).

It was easy to sneak out. Mom was in deep conversation with Pilar in the kitchen. I think Pilar may come back to work.

When Ducky and I arrived at Rico's, the whole group looked played-out and tired. James was throwing a tantrum, ranting about how they'd never be ready in only one week.

One week.

I knew I was to blame. I'd ruined the rehearsal by being late.

I quickly grabbed my tambourine. The band started playing "Fallen Angel." I tried to sing, but my voice was constricted and weak.

By the end of rehearsal, I wanted to cry. But I held back my tears while we agreed on a rehearsal schedule.

Now I'm committed to tomorrow, Friday, Saturday, Sunday, and Monday.

Five days out of six. I get Thanksgiving off. (Thanksgiving — I haven't even *thought* about it!) I don't know how I'm going to do this.

I was a nervous wreck when I got home. Mom nonchalantly asked where I'd been. I nonchalantly mumbled something about a We ♥ Kids Club meeting.

She totally fell for it. Despite the fact that the We ♥ Kids Club has been practically defunct for ages.

What is happening to me?

I'm useless.

I can't sing.

I can't keep up my grades.

And I'm a liar.

I might as well fall asleep and not wake up.

Slow down,
Way down.
What goes round
comes round.
Dry your eyes,
Clear your mind
You just gotta take it
One day at a time.
Years from now
What'll you say?
"I tried my best" or
"I threw it all away"?
Life has no guarantees
It's a roll of the dice;
So do it all,
Pay the price,
But dust off your heart
Take it off the shelf;
And don't forget
To love yourself.
Just slow Down,
Way down.

Slow Down,
Way down.

Wednesday 11/26
study hall

I got a 95 on the social studies test.
I think I should have my head examined.

Wednesday
6:57 P.M.

At rehearsal today I sounded fine. A
little hoarse, a little nervous, but fine.

When I arrived home, Zeke held his nose.

"What's wrong with you?" I asked.

"You're sweaty," he said. "I hate B.O. Do
you have a boyfriend or something?"

"*What?*"

"Why else would you get so sweaty? You
must have been making out."

I refused to dignify that.

I went upstairs and freshened up.

My hair looked awful. All flyaway and stringy.

I am so sick of long hair. I must do something about it.

Shaving it off might be nice.

That would be a Look.

Friday 11/28
4:34 P.M.

I have an idea.

For a Look, I mean. During yesterday's Thanksgiving dinner, I felt like a total prisoner. I figure I can shave my head, wear horizontal stripes, and be sort of a human beachball.

I mentioned this to Sunny, Dawn, and Ducky today. Sunny practically squealed with excitement.

"You *have* to do it!" she said.

"I was kidding," I insisted.

"You have a gorgeous head shape," Sunny exclaimed.

"You could just cut it really short," Ducky suggested.

"Like a buzz cut," Sunny said.

"I think," Dawn announced, "that to find a new Look, we should go to the source of all new Looks. The mall."

Off we went.

We sat around the fountain and observed the huge post-Thanksgiving mob. We hung out near the hairstylist. We went into the magazine shop and looked at fashion magazines.

Sunny thinks I should go with green makeup and white, spiky hair.

Dawn prefers the barefoot, no-makeup, natural-girl look.

Ducky likes cat's-eye glasses, flats, and a neon fifties dress.

I bought a bunch of possible outfits. One from Column A, one from Column B, one from Column C.

And I am more confused than ever.

I *still* haven't decided on a Look.

It may not matter. I may not be able to sing on Tuesday anyway. I think I have a node on my throat.

I don't know what that means exactly, but toward the end of rehearsal tonight I was totally hoarse, and James said, "You sound like you have a node."

He said I have to get lots of sleep, drink tea with honey, and not speak under any circumstances.

Which made dinner a little difficult.

I pointed to what I needed. I wrote messages. I claimed I had laryngitis. I drank a quart of orange juice.

Luckily Mom and Dad aren't home. Dad's still at the office and Mom's at a dinner party.

Pilar's back, though (yea!), and seemed amused. She called me Harpo. (Zeke called me Farto and thought he was being quite clever, but I ignored him.)

Now I am in bed. Zeke is playing video games with some friend. Pilar is baby-sitting.

If any of them try to find me, I will be fast asleep.

Good night.

Sunday 11/30
7:50 P.M.

I was too depressed to write yesterday. When I tried to sing at rehearsal, I sounded like a Muppet. So I had to hum.

James and Rico were very patient, but I could see they were worried. I don't blame them.

Today was better. A little. If I sang really close to the mike, I actually made an audible croaking sound.

At the end, James took me aside. He asked would I mind if he took "Hey, Down There" off the set list.

Mind? I didn't even know it was *on* the set list. And I certainly don't want to sing it in public.

So I told him no, I didn't mind at all. And he smiled and called me a good sport.

If only he knew how relieved I felt.

Monday 12/1
7:38 P.M.

Oh no oh no oh no.

What have I done?

I am typing this at my desk, standing up.

I am standing up so I can turn and look at my image.

I am looking at my image because it may be the last time I see myself alive.

If I do not survive the day and someone reads this, I plead insanity. I had another grueling rehearsal and I was tired. So I did not know what I was doing afterward.

A half hour ago I was in the kitchen, helping Pilar clean up. I was stacking the dishwasher, pushing back the locks of hair that kept falling into my face, wishing I had gotten a haircut.

Then I was up here in my room, looking at that hair. Looking at the nice, even, perfect, shoulder-length style. Hanging a little too long and a little limp, but still neat. Neat and nice.

I began imagining.

I pictured it gone. I tried to feel the breezes on my bare neck. On my ears.

My soul filled with happiness.

So I grabbed a pair of scissors from my desk.

I held out a strand. I opened the blades.

But my fingers stayed put.

I knew I could not do this. Not to my own hair. It was insane. Better idea: call Dawn and Sunny. Ask their advice. Have Ducky drive me to a hairstylist, at least. Someone must still be open.

Then I snapped the blade shut.

A clump of hair fell to my dresser table.

Perfect, blonde hair that spilled like a pile of straw.

Then I took another snip.

And another.

I should have been horrified but I wasn't. I started laughing. *Laughing.*

I just kept going. A couple of inches at first. Then a little more.

First one side, then the other.

I went a little overboard on the left side. It's about, oh, two inches long.

The right side still drapes over my eyes. I was going to cut that, even it all out.

But I didn't. I left it.

I'm tired of being symmetrical.

Total insanity.

So now I look like

Like a

I just don't understand how I

THE BATTLE OF THE BANDS IS TOMORROW! *AND I LOOK LIKE HELL!*

Monday
8:32 P.M.

Okay. Emergency mode.

I made some phone calls.

Ducky's driving over. He's going to pick up Amalia, Sunny, and Dawn on the way.

Meanwhile, my head is in a kerchief. I cannot look at what I did. I am shivering.

I am alive.

Somehow I have survived the night.

Ducky arrived about 15 minutes after I called. I heard voices in the living room. I tried to wrap my hair in a towel, so it would look as if I'd just stepped out of the shower. But the towel kept falling off.

It didn't matter. Ducky, Sunny, Dawn, and Amalia managed to talk their way past Pilar without my help.

They barged into my room, all wide-eyed.

"If you laugh at me, I will never speak to any of you again," I said.

No one laughed.

For a moment, no one said a word. They all just looked.

I grabbed my kerchief.

Sunny reached out to stop me. "Don't! It looks great, Maggie."

"You're lying!" I was hysterical. Almost screaming.

"Okay, *good,* then," Sunny said. "It looks

good. A little ragged, maybe. I can trim the edges."

As she reached for the scissors, Dawn gently turned me toward the mirror. "Maggie, you *do* look good. I like the cut."

"Really?" I asked.

"Me too," Ducky said. "It's cool."

"Absolutely," Amalia reassured me.

I watched as Sunny carefully snipped away some uneven edges. She kept the left and right side asymmetrical but somehow made the whole effect better. As if it had been done *on purpose.*

I was still shell-shocked. But I was getting used to it.

The four of them stuck around for an hour or so. We decided that with the Battle of the Bands less than a day away, I needed a good night's sleep. Therefore, I should wait until morning to show my face around the house.

So when they said good-bye, they scurried out of the house by themselves.

I stared at myself for a long time afterward.

I had to admit, Sunny had done a great job.

I struck a few singing poses. I tried on some of the outfits I'd bought.

The cat's-eye glasses, flats, and retro neon dress did the trick. I looked so strange. Like a character from a fifties science-fiction B-movie.

Well, a fat version of the character. But it was the best I could do.

This morning I was very cautious, though. I waited until the last possible minute before I went to breakfast.

Zeke was the first to see me. He choked on his Froot Loops.

Mom and Dad were in the kitchen, already clearing their plates.

Mom gasped.

Dad almost dropped his plate on the floor.

"Eeeewwwwww," Zeke cried out. "You look *disgusting*!"

"What did you do?" Mom asked.

Her voice was raspy and low-pitched. Her eyes were bloodshot. Hangover alert. Bad news for me.

I tried to act as if nothing unusual had happened. "I guess you don't like it," I said, grabbing a box of cereal and a bowl from the kitchen.

Mom threw up her hands and walked away. "She's at it again. She's regressed."

I slammed my bowl on the table. "I haven't regressed. I just wanted a new hairstyle for tonight."

That was the truth. Even though our concepts of "tonight" weren't quite the same.

"So you had to do it yourself?" Mom said. "You couldn't go to a salon? What am I going to tell people? All our friends are going to be at the party. The entire industry."

"You don't have to tell them anything," I said. "*I'm* the one with the haircut. Not you."

Mom stormed away.

Dad sat at the table. He looked tired. I could tell he was trying his hardest not to lose his temper.

He told me he was more concerned about my attitude, not my haircut.

"*You're* the one with the attitude

problem these days!" I shouted. (I still can't believe I said that.)

But Dad just nodded sadly. "I know I've been hard to live with lately. My workload has put pressure on you. But you mustn't feel the need to lash out by —"

"I'm not lashing out," I protested. "I just want to look less conservative. Look, if Mom thinks I'll ruin the family image or something, maybe I just shouldn't go tonight."

"I understand what you're going through, Maggie. Really. I mean, we lived through your other phase, right? We can live through this. And don't worry about Mom. She's cranky this morning because she's not feeling well. She's thrilled we'll all be together tonight. So am I. Just promise me you'll work hard to make this a pleasant experience."

"I will."

For as long as I'm there, I didn't say.

It is now 2:11. T minus 5 hours and counting.

I cannot think.

I am shaking.

My fingers are stumbling over the keyboard.

I have never been so nervous in my life.

Just back from our final rehearsal.

Good news item number one: My voice is back. 100%. For what it's worth.

Good news item number two: Everyone in the group LOVES the haircut. And the outfit. James said he was relieved. He didn't think I had it in me to look cool.

I think he was kidding.

Finally, good news item number three: Amalia told me that James told her that Justin Randall is going to be in the audience at Backstreet.

He is going to see me. With my haircut.

He is going to hear my voice.

Maybe this is actually bad news item number one.

My stomach is twisted in knots. What if he hates my look? What if he can't stand my singing?

I can't think about this right now.

It's time.

I have changed into my black dress. My premiere outfit. It looks kind of weird with my haircut, but I can't do anything about that now.

At the Vanish rehearsal, I packed my Battle of the Bands outfit into a shoulder bag, which Amalia will keep.

Ducky will pick her up, along with Sunny and Dawn. Then he will drive all the way to the theater. Just before the 6:15 screening time, I will sneak out of the building and into his car.

One moment I feel exhilarated. Tingly. The next moment I feel like a traitor to my family.

Outside my room, I hear the sounds of total chaos. Dad is rampaging around. He can't find his gold cuff links. Mom is yelling at Zeke because he has chewed up the cuffs of his Brooks Brothers shirt.

I will pack up this laptop now. I will take it with me in its case. I told Mom and Dad I'd be writing a newspaper article on the premiere, and I can't go back on that now.

Probably the next words out of my fingers will be written either in the theater or Backstreet.

If I don't collapse from frayed nerves before then.

Tuesday
6:23 P.M.

I lied. I'm in Ducky's car.

Hi.

Greetings.

YO/ VANISHH RULEZ!!!!!!!!!!

My friends are stealing my Powerbook. That first greeting above was from Dawn. The second was from Amalia, and the third was from Sunny.

Ducky says hi too, but he can't reach the keyboard because he's driving.

They all think I'm insane for bringing this with me.

I don't care. It's the only thing that'll keep me from *going* insane.

OH YOUR FRTIENDS ARENT ENUF HUH?

Above comments (and typos) courtesy of guess who?

This is fun.

I am having the time of my life.

I am also scared out of my wits.

But I did it. I escaped.

It wasn't easy. Nothing about tonight was.

Back at the house, Dad was more frantic than I'd ever seen him. On the way out to the limo, he didn't even seem to notice I was there.

Mom and Zeke took forever to emerge from the house. Zeke was wearing a navy blue suit and looked miserable. Mom's slinky gold dress was dazzling, but she seemed fed up with Zeke.

"Don't you have a nice hat you can wear?" she said to me as she climbed into the limo.

Zeke, to my great surprise, stuck up for me. He said I looked cool. I nearly fainted.

Off we went. Our driver was new, and he got lost. Dad started yelling at him.

Zeke untied his tie. He kept trying to take off his jacket. He complained about everything. I thought Mom was going to throttle him.

Eventually he gave up, and we all fell into a stone-cold silence.

As we approached the theater, I felt as if I were already watching a movie, split screen. Outside was the circus — the spotlights swiveling, the media cameras, the swarms of swanky people. Inside was the Ice Cave of Blume.

We had to wait for another limo to pull away from the curb before we pulled up. As usual, a throng of media people closed around us, trying to gaze through the tinted glass, pushing their cameras toward us.

Then, also as usual, when they realized we were only semifamous, they broke away for the next limo.

I will never understand how Mom and Dad can turn on the smiles in situations like this. They looked as if they'd just been through the happiest day of their lives.

Meanwhile, I was sweating. Trembling. I thought my legs would give out. I felt like a prisoner waiting for the Big Escape.

I stayed with Mom and Dad. I walked into the theater lobby. I said hi to a few people I vaguely knew. I pretended to have some refreshments. Zeke found his friend Randy and went to play the arcade games near the popcorn stand.

And I carefully watched Mom and Dad being swallowed into the crowd.

At 6:05 the lights were dimmed a couple of times. The signal to go inside and sit.

Time for me to sneak away.

My muscles seized up.

I was sure — positive — I'd be caught.

But then I remembered two premieres ago — or was it three? — when I was separated from Mom and Dad in the crowd, and I sat with Monica Kritchman's family. Mom and Dad hadn't minded that a bit. We met up after the film and went merrily home.

The crowd was thinning out in the lobby, all pressing against the entrance doors now. Zeke was still at the arcade games with Randy, oblivious.

Or so I thought.

As I edged toward the door, I heard him cry out, "Hey! Why aren't you with Mom and Dad?"

I asked him the same question, and he said they agreed to let him sit with Randy's family.

I was stuck. I pulled Zeke aside. "Can you keep a secret to your dying day?"

Zeke nodded eagerly.

"My friend Ducky is driving me to a place called Backstreet —"

"For the Battle of the Bands? Cool! But Mom and Dad will notice."

"Not if I'm back for the party. Promise?"

"Promise."

I love my brother.

I kissed him on the forehead and slipped out of the theater.

At first I didn't see Ducky's car. I nearly panicked.

Then I heard it. He had put the Vanish tape on his stereo and cranked it up all the way. I could hear Sunny and him singing along at the top of their lungs.

I have never run so fast. I jumped into the car and did not look back.

And now we are speeding down the Santa Monica Freeway.

Destination Backstreet.

AAAAAAAAAAAAAA!
YEEEEEAAAAAAAAAAAAAAAAAAAAAAAAAAA-
AAAAAAAAAAAAAAAAAAAAAAAAA!
i PRIED sUNNY'S HAND OFF THE a BUTTON
I fixed the caps lock.
WHAT DO I CARE?
I DON'T CARE!
I

I almost erased that entry. But looking at it made me laugh.

That's a good enough reason to keep it.

I was so happy then. We were all ecstatic.

It seems like decades ago.

I know it's late, but I want to recreate the whole wild and weird evening before I forget a moment of it.

By tomorrow, I may not believe it happened.

If it really did.

Even now, it all feels like a dream.

We reached Backstreet around 6:50. The place was packed. People were lined up outside the door. Inside, another group's music was blasting away.

I should have been absolutely stiff with fear. But I wasn't. Something came over me. A feeling I never expected.

It was the strangest thing. As I left the car, clutching the shoulder bag that contained my clothes, I felt as if a gust of air were carrying me toward the entrance. Each step made me stronger. I was soaking up the energy. Letting it charge me like a battery.

A surly, muscle-bound guy was standing

guard. I walked right up to him and said, "Blume. Vocalist for Vanish. Four guests."

He checked a list and waved us in.

The room was jammed. A thicket of people hid the bar to our left. Further in, waiters swarmed around small tables, each of which held many more people than it was meant to. Laughter and shouting seemed to clog the air. The air-conditioning must have been blasting all day, because the place was freezing.

James was at the far end, waving to me.

I let Ducky lead the way through the room. James greeted us with an amazed look. "Rico's throwing up," he said. "From excitement. He's *happy* and he's puking."

"Lovely," I said. "I refuse to share a mike with him."

A joke.

I had a sense of humor.

I was loose. *Calm.*

We all slipped through a door, into a grimy backstage area with peeling stucco walls. Musicians were milling around, tuning instruments, chatting. Bruce and Patti were jamming a blues riff in a corner.

I said hi and quickly ran to the bathroom to change. By the time I got back, all made up and ready to go, Rico was tuning his guitar. He looked a little pale but he was beaming nevertheless.

"We're on third," James said. "We were supposed to be seventh, but I knew you had to go, Maggie, so I traded."

I kissed him. Amalia didn't mind.

"Oh, one other thing," James began.

"*LET'S HEAR IT FOR BACKSTREET'S ANNUAL BATTLE OF THE BANDS!*" an amplified voice blared out.

James never did finish. We were all whooping and cheering.

I don't remember a thing about the first and second groups. I don't remember much about the wait at all — just the sound of that voice again, this time shouting: "*And now, from the streets of Palo City, let's give it up for . . . Vanish!*"

And then I was onstage. Pounding my tambourine. Singing. Feeling the pulse of the music. Feeling the audience pulse with us. We sang "Hook Shot" and "Fallen Angel" (with *my* words).

As the crowd applauded, I reached for my maracas for "Calico Rat Love Blues," which was next. I heard Bruce playing the bass line for "Hey, Down There," just fooling around, and I smiled.

As I stood up, James leaned over to me. "Put those away. We're doing 'Hey, Down There.'"

I thought he was joking. I laughed.

"Go ahead," he urged, pointing to the keyboard.

No joke. My insides were suddenly having a seismic shift. "That's not on the set list!" I said.

"That's what I was starting to tell you backstage. We changed it back."

"But —"

The crowd was quieting down. Bruce, Patti, and Rico were all looking at me to start.

Sweat began pouring out of my neck like a lawn sprinkler.

I sidled over to the keyboard. I took a deep breath. I nodded to Bruce, and he started the bass line again. For real.

Looking out into the crowd, I saw a sea of eyes like little lanterns staring at me.

And then I recognized two of those lanterns.

They belonged to Justin Randall. And they were trained on me.

My fingers weighed about three tons. They stayed on my lap when I was supposed to begin playing. Bruce vamped on the bass for another four measures.

I turned away from Justin and looked at the keys. I saw my hands putting themselves into position, as if they had a mind of their own.

Suddenly I was filled with gratitude to Mrs. Knudsen, of all people. The eight years of Chopin and Mozart and Beethoven animated my fingers. Made them go to the right notes, even though my brain was trying desperately to run away.

"Hey . . . down there . . ."

A voice.

Mine. It was coming out before I knew what I was doing.

I closed my eyes and thought about the song. Nothing but the song.

The song that I had written with Justin Randall in mind.

"Why do you look at me the way you do . . . ?"

When I opened my eyes, all I could see was Justin. As if the whole audience had merged into one face.

An unrecognizable sound came out of my mouth. Somewhere between a squeak and a bleat, on the high note.

I averted my eyes. I found Amalia and looked at her.

Soon I wasn't seeing anyone's face at all. The crowd seemed to blur and fade. The sounds of clinking glasses, the heat of the lights, the sensation of my fingers pounding and my voice reaching — all gone, all absorbed into the rhythm and words. As if the song itself had taken charge of my senses.

"Hey . . . down there . . . I love you."

And then the song was over. I held the final note and let my hands rest on the chord until the sound faded away.

I had gotten through it. I don't know how. I was dazed.

I could hear plenty of applause, and that was nice. But no one was calling for an encore. The only people standing and shouting were Amalia, Marina, Cece, Dawn, Ducky, and Sunny.

And Justin.

He was grinning at me. He lifted his fingers to his mouth and let out a loud, enthusiastic whistle.

And that was it. End of set. A moment to bow, a loud send-off by the announcer, and the next group began setting up behind us.

The moment we were backstage, all the tension rushed out of me. I screamed.

I felt so happy.

I hugged James. Then Rico hugged us. Before we knew it, all five of us were one mass hug, staggering across the floor, laughing hysterically.

We shrieked out congratulations into each other's ears. Everyone told me how well my song went.

When the other group started, we shut up and watched them.

All the while, I was having the weirdest sensation. Like two voice tapes running simultaneously inside my head. One voice telling me I was not perfect. Reminding me of the botched entrance to "Hey, Down

There." The squeak. The rhythm I'd messed up during "Fallen Angel." A couple of other missed cues.

I know that voice. It's there when I take my exams. When I turn in a paper. When I play a piano piece. When I dress myself in the morning.

Always.

It's me. The voice of Maggie.

It was dawning on me how strong that voice is.

No, not just strong. More than that.

It runs my life.

But at that moment, it wasn't. Because another voice was telling me something else. That the mistakes didn't matter. That winning the contest would be nice but who cared?

That I'd done something worth doing. Something that *I* wanted to do.

Not for grades.

Not for my permanent record.

Not for Dad or the five-year plan.

For me.

I was in the middle of all these thoughts when a hand landed on my shoulder.

I turned, and Ducky folded me into yet another hug, which Amalia joined, along with Cece and Marina — and then Dawn and Sunny.

As I rocked back and forth, listening to them compliment me, I saw Justin.

He was standing behind my friends, smiling.

"Nice song," he said.

"Thanks." That was all I managed to utter before Ducky was dragging me toward the exit.

"Hey! Stop!" I said.

"Come on, Cinderella!" he was shouting. "It's pumpkin time."

"But — but —" I stammered.

Justin had this bewildered look on his face. He wanted to talk to me more. I could tell.

"Don't worry about Amalia and Sunny and those guys. They're going to catch a ride home later," Ducky insisted. "We have to go!"

I almost screamed at Ducky. I almost told him he was dense. But then I looked at my watch.

Ducky was right.

My shoulder bag was against the wall

where I'd left it. I quickly took it into the bathroom and changed back to my black dress.

As I darted out, I could see Amalia, Cece, Dawn, and Sunny chatting away.

Justin was in the midst of friends too. But he was looking right at me.

Smiling.

I did the only thing I could do. I waved good-bye.

Ducky was waiting in his car at the curb as I raced outside. I jumped in and we took off.

We floated down the freeway. Ducky launched into the story of how he "accidentally" spilled soda on a guy at the next table who wouldn't shut up. I told him about James's last-minute surprise onstage. We could not stop talking and laughing.

And all the while, I kept seeing Justin's smile.

Ducky almost missed our exit because we were screaming the lyrics to "Fallen Angel."

But as we turned onto the city streets, I looked at the time and fell quiet.

"What exact time does the movie end?" Ducky asked.

"I don't know," I said. "Around now."

We hit every single red light. I was a nervous wreck by the time we pulled into the parking lot.

My heart sank when I saw the theater. People were milling around outside it. Some were leisurely walking next door to Duomo.

"Uh-oh," Ducky murmured.

"I hope they haven't been looking for me," I said.

"If you get in there before them, just sit at your table. Tell them you were sitting at the back of the theater during the movie with a friend, and you were hungry. If you want, I'll be that friend. I'll come in with you."

"It's invitation-only," I explained. "They'll ask questions."

Ducky pulled to the front of the restaurant. He shouted good luck as I raced inside.

I pushed open the door and immediately realized that the dining room was absolutely hushed. My heart leaped. I thought I was early.

Then, around a velvet curtain, I saw the tables filled with people. All of them were looking to the left, smiling.

"And if the audience response is any indication, we can look forward to a very exciting first weekend," an amplified voice boomed out.

Dad's voice.

I moved further into the restaurant, past the curtain. Dad was standing at a podium behind a lavish buffet table.

"Now, I know you're all saying to yourselves, 'Can't this guy stop thanking people so we can eat?'" Dad said to a wave of nodding heads and knowing chuckles. "But I would be remiss if I didn't give my deepest thanks to my real collaborators. To my most important partners, not in the movie business, but in life. To the people who've had to put up with me day and night during a tense period . . . whose love makes everything possible . . . my family."

People burst into applause. A spotlight

blinked on and swept to the banquet table in front of Dad.

Pinned by the light, Mom and Zeke stood and waved to the crowd.

Opposite them at the table, surrounded by lots of producers and their families, were two empty seats.

My evening — my glorious, happy, triumphant evening — flew away like an ash from a campfire.

Quickly I made my way through the restaurant toward the Blume family table. When I arrived there, Dad was standing at his seat, chatting with his tennis partner, Carlton Grant.

"Ah, she's here!" Mr. Grant said as he saw me. "How was the performance?"

I nearly passed out. *How did he know?*

"It went really well," I replied, looking at Dad. "You found out?"

Dad's return glance gave me the shivers. He was furious.

"Your dad was telling me all about your debut with the school orchestra," Mr. Grant continued. "Which Brahms piano concerto was it?"

"Uh, the second," I murmured.

So that was it. Dad had lied to cover my absence.

But *a Brahms piano concerto?*

I mean, really. If Dad had to lie, he could have picked something realistic. Something a 13-year-old could actually play.

I let that thought go. Dad wasn't doing anything worse than what I had just done.

As we sat down next to each other, I could practically feel the icy blast coming from Dad. He did not say a word to me. Just grabbed a piece of bread and started chewing. I was surprised he could unlock his jaw to eat.

"Come with me," Mom said to Zeke and me, standing up.

Zeke gave me a Look and drew his finger across his neck to show me how much trouble I was in.

Mom greeted about a dozen people on the way to the buffet table. Her voice was too loud. She was laughing too much. Four drinks, I figured. Her words weren't slurred yet. But she was definitely on her way.

As we stood over a steaming tray of

pasta, Mom said through gritted teeth, "Did you have a good time?"

I nodded. I could feel tears starting to well up.

"I had assumed you were with the Kritchmans," Mom continued. "I didn't spot them until after the movie was over. They didn't know where you were. Thank goodness for Zeke. *He* knew."

I glared at Zeke. "Thanks a lot."

"They made me tell!" Zeke protested.

"Don't be snide with him," Mom said. "If he hadn't said something, we'd have called the police. Now, I would appreciate it if you'd take your food to the table and do your father and me the favor of not mentioning this incident at all until we go home."

I swallowed my tears.

That was about all I *could* swallow. I wasn't hungry at all.

Later, while Mom and Dad were drinking coffee, I called Amalia. She told me Vanish had won second place. Even that news didn't lift my mood.

I hardly said a word all night, even

after we climbed into the limo for the trip home.

Zeke kept up a steady stream of chatter, reciting various bits from the movie. Mom kept trying to talk, but she wasn't making much sense. Dad sat there like a stone, ignoring everything.

Before long, both Mom and Zeke were zonked out.

As we glided along the freeway, the limo felt more like a hearse. Finally, halfway home, Dad spoke up. "That will never, *ever* happen again."

I nodded, cringing inside.

I wanted so much to explain. To tell him what I'd been through. To let him know how important it all was.

But I knew he'd never understand.

So I just apologized a hundred times, fell silent again, and watched a falling tear disappear into the carpet.

"How'd the group do?" Dad asked.

I looked up at him. His face had softened a little. He was sitting back, his eyes narrowed.

"Second place," I said.

Dad raised his eyebrows. "Second place," he repeated with a nod. Then he stared out the window.

I felt a wave of relief. He seemed kind of impressed.

But I know Dad. And I could tell from his voice that he would have been happier if I'd said first place.

Which made me feel a small knot in my stomach.

Because now, looking back at the performance, I knew I agreed with him. I'd have been happier too.

I'm feeling that way right now.

I have been trying to recapture how I felt at Backstreet. I can, sort of. The joy is still with me. I'm still proud of myself.

But I can't help thinking: What would have happened if I hadn't squeaked? Or if I'd made all my cues? Or if I hadn't forced Bruce to vamp on that song entrance?

Could we have made first place?

I guess I'll never know.

But I do know one thing. I can't stop. I

can't stop writing. Or singing. I can't stop trying for first. In *something.*

Dad can control a movie studio. He can wrap major stars around his finger. But he doesn't know me. And he can't control what he doesn't know.

Someday he'll get it. Someday he'll see me on the Grammies. Or he'll watch me accept the Pulitzer. Or maybe he'll drop by my very own animal hospital. And I'll smile at him. And he won't be mad at me anymore.

In the meantime I'll stick with my friends who *do* get it. Sunny, Amalia, Dawn, Ducky — they've all seen the real me. So has Justin.

Does he get it?

He must. He wouldn't have given me that smile for no reason at all.

Tomorrow I have to talk to him. I have to find out.

If I ever, *ever* get to sleep . . .

L. GODWIN

Ann M. Martin

About the Author

ANN MATTHEWS MARTIN was born on August 12, 1955. She grew up in Princeton, NJ, with her parents and her younger sister, Jane.

Although Ann used to be a teacher and then an editor of children's books, she's now a full-time writer. She gets the ideas for her books from many different places. Some are based on personal experiences. Others are based on childhood memories and feelings. Many are written about contemporary problems or events.

All of Ann's characters are made up. But some of her characters are based on real people. Sometimes Ann names her characters after people she knows; other times she chooses names she likes.

In addition to California Diaries, Ann Martin has written many other books, including the Baby-sitters Club series. She has written twelve novels for young people, including *Missing Since Monday, With You or Without You, Slam Book,* and *Just a Summer Romance.*

Ann M. Martin does not live in California, though she does visit frequently. She lives in New York with her cats, Gussie and Woody. Her hobbies are reading, sewing, and needlework — especially making clothes for children.

I grab my drawing out of his hand. "Are you happy now?"

"Sorry, Amalia. I just thought you were keeping secrets from me."

"Even if I <u>was</u>, so what?" I'm almost shouting now. "Do you have to know everything about me?"

"I said I'm sorry." James tries to put his arm around me. "How come you never told me you were so talented?"

He's smiling at me, but now <u>I'm</u> furious. "You think you can just make everything better, just by complimenting me?"

"Whoa. Come on, Amalia, it's not such a big deal."

"Like, I'm so in love with you I'll

let you insult me and be suspicious and accuse me of being in love with everybody in the world and insult my friends and then expect me to forgive you and act like I'm your girlfriend? Why? Just because you're sixteen?"

"Uh, slow down," James says. "What are you saying? You're not my girlfriend?"

My jaw is hanging open, Nbook. It's like he hasn't heard one word of what I've said.

"Stick to girls your own age," I mutter.

I turn. Then I walk around the garage, around the house, and all the way to a corner gas station, where I call home.

A few minutes later, Isabel picks me up. I am crying and she asks why.

I tell her I've broken up with a guy who wasnt even really my boyfriend.

Amalia. Her boyfriend loves her so much, he won't let go.

Tuesday

Before, it was No Big Deal. James wanted to do things his way, and sometimes I let him. But now he won't give up. I don't think I know him anymore. And I'm sure he doesn't know me. What am I going to do?

From the new series by
ANN M. MARTIN

California Diaries

California Diaries #4: AMALIA
Coming to your bookstore this November.

CD497